Also by Joan and Richard Hewett

MOTORCYCLE ON PATROL
ON CAMERA

Laura Loves Horses

By JOAN HEWETT
Photographs by
RICHARD HEWETT

CLARION BOOKS
New York

Clarion Books
a Houghton Mifflin Company imprint
215 Park Avenue South, New York, NY 10003
Printed in Italy
Library of Congress Cataloging-in-Publication Data
Hewett, Joan.
  Laura loves horses / by Joan Hewett; photographs by Richard Hewett.
  p.   cm.
  Summary: Text and pictures follow an eight-year-old Hispanic
girl living on a Southern California horse ranch where her father
works, as she improves her horsemanship and begins to compete
in horse shows.
  ISBN 0-89919-844-9
  [1. Horsemanship—Fiction.]   I. Hewett, Richard, ill.   II. Title.
PZ7.H4485Lau   1990
[Fic]—dc20   89-34987   CIP   AC

NWI 10 9 8 7 6 5 4 3 2 1

For Ann Troy, with love

*B*etween the ocean and the sun-brown southern California hills, trim stables and riding rings stand on a creek-fed slip of land. Eight-year-old Laura Santana and her family live in a small house next to the stables.

Laura's dad, Julio, works on the ranch. He keeps up the grounds and the stables. Close to thirty horses are boarded here: dark Arabians, chestnut Thorough-breds, dappled gray quarter horses…. Early in the morning, Laura pulls on a sweatshirt and slips out the front door to visit them.

The sweet, familiar smell of fresh hay and horses welcomes her. She strokes Perriwinkle's soft muzzle and says hello to Ham and Rosie. Sugar Baby whinnies when Laura reaches her stall. Of all the horses, Sugar is the only one who returns the girl's greeting. She is the first horse Laura was allowed to ride, and they are old friends.

Today is Saturday. They can go to the creek.

Laura gets the pony ready, gathers the reins, and, using a tree stump as a step, hoists herself up on the mare's broad, comfortable back.

It is a slow day. A lazy day. They ramble down the fence-lined road. Then Laura shortens the reins, leans forward, and signals the pony to trot.

Sugar Baby's response is quick, her pace brisk. Laura smiles. She posts in rhythm, up-down, up-down. Clip-clop, clip-clop go the pony's hooves. They are partners heading toward adventure. And there is the creek. Shining.

Shallow water ripples over smooth, fat stones. Sugar Baby feels her way, slowly. "Good girl, good girl," Laura croons. Then they are out in the deep. Splashing.... Racing....

In late summer when the creek is low, Laura and Sugar Baby take a trail that winds through the hills. A red-tailed hawk soars. Saddle-high grass spreads before them.

Sugar halts near a tender clump she would like to munch. She plants her feet stubbornly. Silly old girl, Laura thinks as she guides her on. Then she tickles the pony in a favorite spot below her forelock, and with a "Hi ho, let's go," they canter back to the stables.

Laura dismounts. She walks her hot, sweaty pony round the paddock area, and, after Sugar Baby has cooled off, Laura gives her a juicy apple and returns her to the stall. Then she answers the barn phone, helps groom a friend's horse, and, when there is no more to do, skips off to the riding ring where Kim is teaching.

Laura watches Kim give one riding lesson after another. When the last lesson is over, Kim says, "Time to saddle up," and Laura, Kim, and two other riders are on their way.

Past the creek they follow a narrow trail as it slices through junglelike brush, and, suddenly, they are in a clearing.

Cantering. Galloping. Go, Sugar Baby, go, Laura urges silently.

After a while, horses and riders stop to rest. Laura tries making friends with Fred, Kim's lordly steed. She talks to him softly, and the big Thoroughbred lets Laura stroke his light chestnut coat.

Although Fred is not really a "people" horse, he follows Kim's commands and performs well in shows. Kim will be riding in a horse show next week. So will Laura.

When Laura was little, she watched the stable hands ready horses for showing. They groomed them till they shone, braided their manes, loaded them on trailers.... Laura wondered what a horse show was like.

Then Kim taught Laura how to ride English style. Laura practiced continually, and one day Kim offered to let her ride Perriwinkle and learn to jump.

Laura could barely believe it. She longed to jump, and Perriwinkle, a high-spirited but gentle Thoroughbred–quarter horse, would be wonderful to ride. Listening to Kim carefully, she put the lively mare through her paces: walk, trot, and canter. Then they neared the first hurdle, Perri's muscles rippled and gathered, and the next moment they were soaring up and over.

Now, two months and several lessons later, Laura
is entering her first horse show. It is a three-day
American Horse Shows Association competition.

The Equestrian Center seems like some kind of
medieval encampment. Riders and stables display their
colors and insignias. Gleaming, smooth steeds with
finely braided manes poke their heads from adjacent
stalls. Nostrils flaring, an excited mount snorts. And
over the sounds of a milling crowd, a roll call of names
summons the waiting riders.

There will be many events, called classes, and a lot of riders competing in each one. Laura will be riding hunter class for children age twelve and under. She tries to look calm like the more experienced riders, but her heart thumps as she changes into her full riding habit.

Kim helps smooth Laura's hair so her helmet will fit. Then one of the other riders pins the number 175 to the back of Laura's jacket. It will be Laura's number for the entire show.

Different classes are going on in different rings. Laura watches advanced riders school their horses over four-foot jumps.

Children's hunters over fences will be Laura's first class. There will be eight, three-foot fences. With Kim by her side, Laura walks the course, pacing the distance between each jump.

Laura starts feeling shaky; if only the waiting would end.... At last it is time to warm up, and there is Perri. Beautiful Perri, dark and swift and sleek. Laura takes a deep breath. She will not be timid. This is a time to be brave.

Some of the riders Laura will be competing with are already in the schooling area. Perri seems glad to warm up. She responds promptly and takes each jump with even strides.

The paddock master calls the riders to the ring. Riders will go through the course in turn. Laura watches each contender. Finally, she moves up to the starting gate. "We're next," she whispers to Perri.

28

And then she hears the call—"Number 175, Laura Santana riding Perriwinkle."

Laura signals and they are off. With easy grace and a light, steady hand, she guides Perri through the course. The first jump is straight ahead. They take it smoothly, and the next, and the next....

Then in a wink they are
finished. Laura gives Perri
a big thank-you kiss. The
last rider completes the
course. The judge names the
winners. Laura has come in
third. She's won a yellow
ribbon!

Laura has now ridden in many horse shows. Still, she loves to rise early on a Saturday morning, pull on old clothes, and make her way to the stables. She visits Perri, Fred, and some of the other horses. Then she saddles Sugar Baby, and they ride past the ranch and through the creek.

Sometimes Laura and a friend ride together. A stiff breeze filled with the heady smell of ocean and adventure lures them on. They gallop their horses to the water's edge, then race through the surf and dodge the waves.

Before they head
back, Laura leans over
and rests her damp face
close to Sugar Baby's.
"You're my girl," she tells
the pony. "You're the
best."

ACKNOWLEDGMENTS

Our thanks to: Bob Williams, owner of Sycamore Farm, for his kind and generous cooperation, and Kim Overholt, Sue Overholt, Robert Peters, Jr., Melissa Glenn, and Ann Whitford Paul for their valuable assistance, and Patricia Ridgeley and Darlene Sordillo for leading us to Laura. A special thanks to Laura's parents, Julio and Victoria Santana, for their gracious aid, and to Laura for her unflagging enthusiasm. We would also like to recognize and thank the owners of Zulika Farms for their all important support, and Ann Troy, our editor, for her freely given encouragement and faith.